P9-CBP-218

MY FIRST

I Can Read Book®

Bathtime for Biscuit

SCHOOL DIST. 106
2165 TELEGRAPH ROAD
DEERFIELD, ILLINOIS 60015

by ALYSSA SATIN CAPUCILLI
pictures by PAT SCHORIES

HarperTrophy®
A Division of HarperCollinsPublishers

Bathtime for Biscuit
Text copyright © 1998 by Alyssa Satin Capucilli
Illustrations copyright © 1998 by Pat Schories
Printed in the U.S.A. All rights reserved.

Library of Congress Cataloging-in-Publication Data
Capucilli, Alyssa.
  Bathtime for Biscuit / story by Alyssa Satin Capucilli ; pictures by
Pat Schories.
      p.   cm. —(A my first I can read book)
  Summary: Biscuit the puppy runs away from his bath with his puppy friend Puddles.
  ISBN 0-06-027937-0. — ISBN 0-06-027938-9 (lib. bdg.)
  ISBN 0-06-444264-0 (pbk.)
  [1. Dogs—Fiction.   2. Baths—Fiction.]   I. Schories, Pat, ill.   II. Title.   III. Series.
PZ7.C179Bat   1998   97-49663
[E]—dc21   CIP
                                                                                                  AC

First Harper Trophy edition, 1999
❖
Visit us on the World Wide Web!
http://www.harperchildrens.com

This one is for my parents.
—A.S.C.

To Sri K.
—P.S.

Time for a bath, Biscuit!

Woof, woof!

Biscuit wants to play.

Time for a bath, Biscuit!

Woof, woof!

Biscuit wants to dig.

Time for a bath, Biscuit!

Woof, woof!

Biscuit wants to roll.

Time for a bath, Biscuit!
Time to get nice and clean.
Woof, woof!

In you go!

Woof!

Biscuit does not want a bath!

Bow wow!
Biscuit sees
his friend Puddles.

Woof, woof!

Biscuit wants to climb out.

Come back, Biscuit!

Woof!

Come back, Puddles!

Bow wow!

Biscuit and Puddles
want to play
in the sprinkler.

18

Biscuit and Puddles
want to dig
in the mud.

Biscuit and Puddles
want to roll
in the flower bed.

Now I have you!

Woof, woof!
Let go of the towel,
Biscuit!

Bow wow!

Let go of the towel,

Puddles!

Silly puppies!

Let go!

Woof, woof!

Bow wow!

Oh!

Time for a bath, Biscuit!

Woof, woof!

A bath for all of us!

BANNOCKBURN SCHOOL DIST. 106
2165 TELEGRAPH ROAD
DEERFIELD, ILLINOIS 60015